THIS WALKER BOOK BELONGS TO:

_____

_____

_____

_____

sleeping

dancing

crying

waving

giving

eating

skipping

telling

listening

thinking

yawning

kicking

smelling

stroking

giving

shouting

washing

writing

singing

tearing

For Mark

First published 1993 by Walker Books Ltd
87 Vauxhall Walk, London SE11 5HJ

This edition published 1995

2 4 6 8 10 9 7 5 3 1

© 1993 Shirley Hughes

This book has been typeset in Plantin.

Printed in Hong Kong

British Library Cataloguing in Publication Data
A catalogue record for this book is
available from the British Library.

ISBN 0-7445-3653-7

Giving

Shirley Hughes

WALKER BOOKS

AND SUBSIDIARIES

LONDON • BOSTON • SYDNEY

I gave Mum a present on her birthday,
all wrapped up in pretty paper.

And she gave me a big kiss.

I gave Dad a very special picture
which I painted at play-group.

And he gave me a ride on his
shoulders most of the way home.

I gave the baby some
slices of my apple.

We ate them sitting under the table.

At teatime the baby gave me
two of his soggy crusts.

That wasn't much of a present!

You can give
someone a
cross look…

or a big smile!

You can give a tea party...

or a seat on a crowded bus.

On my birthday Grandma and Grandpa
gave me a beautiful doll's pram.
I said "Thank you" and gave
them each a big hug.

And I gave my dear Bemily
a ride in it, all the way down the
garden path and back again.

I tried to give the
cat a ride too,

but she gave me a
nasty scratch!

So Dad had to give my poor arm a kiss and a wash and a piece of sticking plaster.

Sometimes, just when
I've built a big castle
out of bricks,

the baby comes along and
gives it a big swipe!
And it all falls down.

Then I feel like giving
the baby a big
swipe too.

But I don't, because

he *is* my baby brother, after all.

sleeping

dancing

crying

waving

giving

eating

skipping

telling

listening

thinking

yawning

kicking

smelling

stroking

giving

shouting

washing

writing

singing

tearing

MORE WALKER PAPERBACKS
For You to Enjoy

Also by Shirley Hughes

BOUNCING / CHATTING / GIVING / HIDING

Each of the books in this series for pre-school children takes a single everyday
verb and entertainingly shows some of its many meanings and applications.

"There's so much to look at, so much to read in
Shirley Hughes' books." *Children's Books of the Year*

0-7445-3652-9   *Bouncing*
0-7445-3654-5   *Chatting*
0-7445-3653-7   *Giving*
0-7445-3655-3   *Hiding*
£3.50 each

OUT AND ABOUT

Eighteen richly-illustrated poems portray the weather and
activities associated with the various seasons.

"Hughes at her best. Simple, evocative rhymes conjure up images that
then explode in the magnificent richness of her paintings." *The Guardian*

0-7445-1422-3   £3.99

TALES FROM TROTTER STREET

"Shirley Hughes is one of the all-time greats and her new series
accurately describes the life of contemporary city kids." *Susan Hill, Today*

0-7445-2032-0   *Angel Mae*
0-7445-2033-9   *The Big Concrete Lorry*
0-7445-2012-6   *Wheels*
0-7445-2357-5   *The Snow Lady*
£3.99 each